Past & Poison

EZRA DAWN

Past & Poison
Ezra Dawn

Cover art created by JeB Designs
jebdesigns@outlook.com

TABLE OF Contents

Note

This book contains a brief chapter from the POV of the villain as well as the POV'S of the main characters like the previous book. Although, I've changed the header from Mysterioso to Assassino on the villain POV chapter this time since that's what Pieire is. A couple sections in the prologue of this book were taken from Blood and Bullets which is why they'll be familiar to you although some slight changes have been made to those bits. I hope you enjoy it.

CHARACTER NAME
Pronunciation

Ever 'Night' Dracovi (Ever, Dray-co-vee)

Vincetti Morrison (Vin-chet-ee, Morrison)

Rodrigo Morrison (Rod-ree-goh, Morrison)

Giovanni Morrison (Gee-oh-vahn-nee, Morrison)

Rosalie Morrison (Rose-ah-lee, Morrison)

Pieire (Pee-air-ray)

Translation

Moya Dusha—Russian for my soul

Tesoro—Italian for sweetheart

Mio Figlio—Italian for my son

L'venok—Russian for little lion

ABOUT THE
Book

(This book is part of a series that revolves around the same couple. It is recommended that you read book one before reading this one.)

Just when you think the war is over...a new villain surfaces.

After successfully dismantling Vincetti's uncle's operation, Ever and Vincetti believe the threat to Vincetti's life is no longer in play. However, that all changes when Ever receives a delivery from someone he never wanted to hear from again.

Having nearly lost Vincetti when he was shot three months before Ever is overprotective of his mate. Not willing to let Vincetti put himself at risk by trying to help track down the delivery's sender, Ever keeps the contents to himself and investigates on his own.

The past always catches up and Ever's has put his mate's life in danger once again. If Ever wants to keep Vincetti alive he needs to play by the enemy's rules or risk losing everything. The question is, will he succeed or will he be too late to save the one person who means the world to him?

(Warning: Contains graphic sexual content, graphic descriptions of violence, and explicit language. Not recommended for those under the age of 18. This book ends on a cliffhanger that leads into the next book.)

CHAPTER ZERO
MEMORIES OF THE PAST
Ever

Becoming an Assassin

Forty Years Ago...

I joined a coven after I moved out of my mother's house and worked my way up to an enforcer position. My mother ended up becoming a member of a coven herself when she became pregnant with my sister and wanted her to grow up around others of her kind with the stability and safety a coven brings. I don't get to see them often because their coven is in Russia while mine is in Las Vegas. The coven I'm part of is under new leadership and headed in a direction I'm not sure I want to be a part of, so when I heard that the vampire council had an enforcer position open up, I decided to come and fight for the position, leaving the coven behind.

I'm not the only vampire who came. There's nine others and we'll be using a tournament style process of elimination. For round one, we'll draw numbered chips and matching numbers determine opponents but only for round one. The winners from round one will fight each other in round two. Since there'll be an odd number of combatants, the odd man out will fight the winner of the first fight in round two and so on, until there's only one left standing.

Once we draw numbers, the tournament begins. I make it all the way to the final round but end up losing because my opponent got in a lucky shot that sent me flying out of the ring. Going out of bounds is an automatic disqualification. I'm disappointed but another position is bound to open up in the future. As I'm leaving the fighting area, a voice from behind me says, "You're a good fighter."

"Thanks."

"You should've won that bout, but I'm glad you didn't."

Turning to face the man, I raise an eyebrow and ask, "Why is that?"

He grins and says, "Because now you're a free agent and I can recruit you. I'm in charge of the paranormal council's assassins. It's more extensive training than what you would've gotten as an enforcer and the pay is triple what your salary would be. So, what do you say? Want to join?"

"Sign me up."

Rule #3 (Addendum): *It's every assassin for himself.*

Walking into the council's headquarters, I head straight for the office of the councilman I'm currently working for. I've been a council assassin for five years now, but I'm starting to dislike being at someone's beck and call. Every time I get called in for a new job it's like I'm a godsdamn guard dog being sicced on the enemy. After this job, I think I'm going to go out on my own so I'm no longer beholden to anyone's rules and orders except my own.

Knocking on the office door, I wait for the councilman to say, "Come in," before I enter. As soon as I walk in, I see he's not alone. There's another man standing in front of the councilman's desk wearing black leather pants, a black muscle shirt, and biker boots. His hair is a mix of bright green and black and not something I've seen before. The man isn't quite as tall as me and is rail thin. When he turns to look at me, I see his eyes are gold and there's a coldness to them that immediately tells me he's dangerous.

Tearing my gaze from him, I focus on the councilman and say, "You have a job for me?"

The councilman grins. "Yes, Night, I do. But the assignment will require more than one assassin, since there's multiple targets."

"Who will I be working with?"

The councilman tips his head towards the man I'm now standing next to and says, "This is Pieire, he'll be joining you on the mission and you'll work as a team. Pieire is one of our recent graduates and was the top of his class. This is his first job, so I trust you'll take him under your wing."

Yeah, there's no chance of that happening since this'll be my last. But I keep that to myself.

Turning toward Pieire, I paste a fake smile on my face, adopt a cordial attitude, hold out my hand and say, "I look forward to working with you."

Pieire takes my hand in his and purrs, "Likewise, little mouse."

Little did I know this meeting and that simple gesture would set off a chain of events that would lead to me living on the run for years.

The Job and the Psychopath From Hell

Thirty-Five Years Ago...

After taking out the two targets I was assigned to, I go to the rendezvous point to meet up with Pieire who's been assigned to two targets of his own. We're supposed to be there at a certain time so we can catch our ride out of here. When I get there, Pieire is standing over a man who's on his back with blood pooling around him. I studied the targets we were both assigned to and I know immediately that the man on the ground wasn't one of them.

"Pieire, what did you do?"

Pieire looks at me with those soulless golden eyes of his and says, "He saw me kill one of the targets and followed me back here. We can't leave any witnesses."

As the man on the ground struggles to breathe, I curse. "Pieire, you didn't have to hurt him! I could've altered his memories and no one would be the wiser."

Pieire smiles wickedly and says, "Where would be the fun in that?"

Jesus, he's a psychopath. The council is going to regret hiring him when he goes off the deep end. Someone who kills for sport is not a person who'll stick to obeying orders for very long. Not when they lack morals. *I'm glad I'm getting out now, because if the council is training more people just like him, I have a feeling the world will be worse off than it already is.* Plus, if I did stick around and had to keep working with people like Pieire it would only be a matter of time before my own morals drive me to wipe out every psychopath the council has on the payroll and land myself in jail *or worse...six feet under.*

When the helicopter taking us out of here arrives, I climb in and put on the headphones. Pieire takes the seat beside me, puts his headphones on, and says into the mic, "I liked working with you, maybe we could do it again sometime."

Making a noncommittal noise, I turn to look out the window as the helicopter lifts into the air. When the helicopter lands an hour and a half later, we transfer to a vehicle to drive the rest of the way to council headquarters. Because council assassins are supposed to be a secret, we can't be dropped off at the building itself, on the off chance someone figures out who was in the helicopter and traced the flight plan to our location.

It's just Pieire and myself in the car, and I chose to drive because the one and only other time I let Pieire drive, he nearly killed us no less than ten times during the short fifteen-minute ride. When Pieire's hand slides up my thigh and lands on my crotch, I glare at him, "What the hell are you doing?"

Pieire smirks at me and says, "If you need to ask, I'm not doing it right."

Grabbing his wrist, I pull his hand away from me and say, "Don't touch me."

"Come on, little mouse, I saw you checking me out when we were paired up. You could easily become an obsession of mine. You're cold, you kill, so you're just like me. Let's have a little fun together."

"No thanks."

The smirk slips off his face and his eyes narrow. "Why not?"

"I don't sleep with coworkers."

"So, quit. We won't be coworkers then."

"While I do plan to quit, the answer is still no."

Pieire tries to grab my crotch again and says, "I bet I could make you change your mind if you give me a chance."

Parking the car in front of council headquarters, I shake my head. "It's not going to happen. While you might be attractive to some people and definitely dress to stand out, you're not my type. Even if I did want to sleep with you, I wouldn't after you killed an innocent man today when there wasn't a need for it. You're a cold-blooded psychopath and unlike you, I have morals. Nothing you do will change my mind."

Exiting the car, I head towards the front door of the building, as Pieire shouts from behind me. "I'll make you regret rejecting me, little mouse!"

A month later, I was on my first job as a hitman for hire in Monaco when the first package arrived. It contained pictures of me at home, out and about, and in compromising positions with a few of my hook-ups. One of the pictures of me on my own had a target drawn on it, with the words 'you will be mine' written in red. That was the day I made the decision to keep an eye on my back. One thing is certain it doesn't matter how far you run the past will always catch up.

Meeting the Devil Again

Thirty Years Ago...

Valentine's day in Paris...how romantic. It's a shame my target will have to miss it. Looking through the scope of my rifle, I make sure the target is centered on his head and pull the trigger. The bullet enters through the window of his kitchen and lodges in his skull. The force of the bullet tearing through his brain sends him flying off his stool to land on the floor in a heap as blood pools around him. Packing up my rifle, I strap the case to my back, climb down the fire escape and swing my leg over the motorcycle I parked there. Pulling on my helmet, I return to the hotel I'm staying at. I still have a few hours before my flight leaves so, I drop my rifle off in the room and go get something to eat that'll tide me over until I'm forced to have a meal on the plane.

This hotel has a restaurant inside it, so I don't have to go far. I could've ordered room service but I'm in the mood to sit in my room alone until it's time to head for the airport. The lunch rush has already come through so getting a table is easy enough. While I'm perusing the menu, a familiar scent hits my nose seconds before a voice to my left says, "Well, well, well, fancy meeting you here, little mouse."

Rolling my eyes, I say, "Yeah…fancy that." I'd seen him around a few times, but always made sure I was going in the opposite direction. *Figures he'd pop up when my appetite is keeping me from leaving.*

Pieire sits in the chair across from me and asks, "Are you here for business or pleasure?"

"Business. Not that it's any of yours."

"Don't be like that little mouse. I'm here on business too."

I'm sure my voice is dripping sarcasm when I say, "Fantastic."

Pieire grins devilishly and says, "You know, my offer still stands."

"Not interested."

"I'll change your mind eventually."

"That's doubtful."

Pieire stands and says, "We'll see about that. I do love a challenge and you're the perfect one. One day, I'll make you mine and then I'll never let you go." With a nod to my food he says, "Enjoy your meal," and walks away.

"You seriously need to get a life," I mutter as he leaves the restaurant.

As soon as he's out of sight, I breathe a sigh of relief. Him being in the same city as me could be a total coincidence but I have my doubts. To be on the safe side, when I get home, I'll move to a new city and abandon my current alias. A decision that's proven to be a good idea when I return to my hotel room after eating and find an envelope waiting for me that's been slid under the door. The pictures inside reveal that Pieire knows where I'm currently living. On the final image, instead of the words 'you will be mine' it says, 'I'll change your mind.' Which means, he left the envelope here after our chat in the restaurant. *Maybe someday, he'll turn his obsession towards someone else and I can finally stop looking over my shoulder all the damn time. One can only hope.*

See You Again

Twenty-Five Years Ago...

When in Rome do as the Romans do...

And...another one bites the dust... Dismantling my rifle, I pack it into my backpack and zip it shut. A man carrying a backpack in a crowd full of tourists is less suspicious to anyone watching on security feeds. The sound of slow clapping from behind me has me tensing. Standing, I sling the bag over my shoulder and turn around slowly keeping one hand on the handgun that's tucked into my waistband. Seeing Pieire standing there I curl my fingers around the gun's grip and flick off the safety. It's loaded, with one in the chamber already; all I have to do is draw it and pull the trigger.

I'm not entirely sure how the bastard keeps finding me. For years, I've gotten packages with pictures and notes sent to me wherever I'm at whether I'm in between jobs or not. It doesn't matter how many times I move he always tracks me down. Just to draw out the torture he only shows up in person once every five years. It's enough to make sure I never forget him. Though I don't see how I could with the shit he sends me all the time.

Pieire crosses over to where I'm standing and says, "Hello little mouse, nice to see you again."

"I wish I could say the same, but I'd be lying."

For a moment his eyes flicker with anger but he quickly masks it. Brushing past him I head for the stairs leading down to the lower levels of the colosseum. Before I reach them Pieire runs ahead and stops in front of me blocking the stairs. "Don't walk away from me little mouse. I only want to talk."

"No thanks. I want nothing to do with you."

Pieire's mouth tilts in a twisted grin when he says, "Funny, your mother and sister had the opposite opinion."

The thought that he was anywhere near my family has me tensing.

"They're such nice people. It'd be a shame if something were to happen to them."

Grabbing his shirt, I slam him into the wall, press the barrel of my gun to his head and say, "You stay away from my family."

"Tsk. Tsk. Is this any way to treat your mate?"

Glaring at him, I snarl, "We aren't mates."

Pieire's grin widens. "That's not what I told your mother. There's no use trying to deny it little mouse. We're inevitable."

Releasing him, I step back and shake my head. "You're delusional."

"You can't run from destiny little mouse. I'm a patient man. You'll be mine eventually."

"I'll never be yours."

Pieire winks and says -after moving away from the wall and stalking toward me a bit.- "We'll see about that. I've told you before I love a challenge. The more you say no the more I want to make you mine. I'll keep coming after you until you give in."

Pieire walks away then he stops and turns to face me. "I'll be sure to tell your mother and sister you say hi next time I see them. You really should visit them more often. Wouldn't want that cute little sister of yours growing up and not knowing who you are."

Shouting, "Stay away from them," I fire a shot at him that he dodges.

With a salute, Pieire says, "Until we meet again, little mouse," and jumps out of the window before I can fire another shot. Crossing over to the window, I see he's rappelled down the side of the colosseum and disappeared into the crowd. *Fuck.* Pulling out my phone, I head for the stairs and dial my mother's number. As soon as she answers she launches into a lecture about how she can't believe I didn't introduce her to my mate myself instead of having the man show up on his own.

"Mom stop yelling and listen to me."

"What is it, *L'venok?*"

"Pieire isn't my mate. He's a psychopath that's fixated on me and will do anything to get what he wants. I need you to take Alice and disappear. Get new identities. Use burner phones. Contact me once a week to check in but toss the phone afterwards and get a new one. Do not under any circumstances tell me where you are or where you're going. The less I know the better. I'm not taking any chances with your safety."

"Surely, he wouldn't do anything to us, right?"

"I don't know but I refuse to take the chance that he would."

"Okay, *L'venok,* we'll go."

"Call me once you get settled."

"I will."

"Stay safe, Mom. I love you."

"Same to you, *L'venok.* Be careful."

Ending the call, I crush the phone and toss it into a trash can on the street then disappear into the crowd.

Return of the Devil
Twenty Years Ago...

_Whiskey in the jar and a head in the box..._The other night, I went to a bar in Belfast after completing a job and ended up meeting the young bartender for a hook-up once the place closed. After a romp between the sheets and wiping his memory of being fed on, I left. Normally, I use bagged blood and keep my hook-ups to blowjobs or hand jobs because I hate meaningless sex and never feel right about leaving someone I liked before they wake up the next morning. Besides my job doesn't allow for deep connections with people because any relationship I have could put the person I'm seeing at risk and I refuse to do that. However, on that night I let the loneliness I've been feeling for the past few years since I sent my family into hiding to keep them safe from Pieire get to me and gave in to temptation. As I cut open the box that was just delivered to my temporary apartment in Dublin and am hit with the smell of old blood when I open the flaps to view the contents I wish I hadn't given in.

Nestled in ice is the severed head of the man I hooked up with. There's a note attached to his forehead with a knife.

YOU'RE MINE

I'LL KILL ANYONE WHO TOUCHES YOU

Beside the man's head is a plastic bag with a folder inside. Pulling the bag out, I open it and take out the folder. Bile rises up in my throat as I flip through the pictures inside. Each photo is timestamped letting me know Pieire grabbed the man shortly after I left him and spent the past two days torturing him before ending the man's life. Each photo is worse than the one before it. By the time I get to the last photo the man has had strips of flesh cut from his body, fingernails pulled before the fingers were cut off, teeth pulled and more. It's the last few photos of how he sexually assaulted the man with a knife before pouring acid over him that has me racing into the bathroom where I lose my breakfast. *Fuck...he didn't deserve this. No one deserves this kind of depravity.* Pieire needs to be stopped. The question is how to accomplish that.

I'd kill him if I could but he's a slippery fucker. Usually, he's long gone by the time I get a lead on where he is after receiving something from him. He's hunting me while I hunt him. Only, I have yet to succeed in locating him before he gets away. I've tried setting traps, but it never works. He's always one step ahead of me. And now I've dragged innocents into this fight because I needed to feel some form of pleasure.

This is a huge escalation from his norm and I have no doubts that any other person I've hooked up with -even if it was just for a blow job or hand job- suffered the same fate as this man. He may not have sent me the photographic evidence because I didn't go very far with the others but I doubt he would've let them go after touching me. It's abundantly clear now that I've gotten this message and seen exactly what he does to anyone who's been intimate with me. Well, never again...I'll condemn myself to a life alone before putting anyone else at risk even if it means rejecting my beloved if I come across them. *At least until I can take care of Pieire.*

I'll disappear again but this time I'll change my tactics to give myself a chance to get him off my back for a while. Hopefully, if it works, I can use the time to gather knowledge and come up with a plan to take him out. A plan that'll be foolproof. When I'm ready to execute said plan, I'll make him come to me and we'll end this once and for all. I don't care how long it takes as long as the end result is the same. Pieire

dead and buried for the things he's done. *And the
predator shall become the prey.*

Found You

Three Months Ago...
Assassino

I look through the scope of my rifle from my position atop the pride's main house and clock Vincetti's position as soon as he enters my line of sight and walks through the front gates. Grinning, I wait until he's close to the house and has a false sense of safety before I take my shot. As soon as he hits the ground, his protector bursts from the trees. I line up a second shot to take out the person I'm being paid extra to kill if he shows himself. My finger freezes on the trigger when my gaze lands on a familiar face. A face belonging to someone I've been trying to track down for years, only to have him stay one step ahead.

"Well, well, well. Looks like I've finally found you, little mouse." *It only took fifteen years of near misses to get to this point.* It was luck that had me catching him in Cairo five years after I sent that gift to him in Dublin. *Kind of like now.*

With a grin, I pack up my rifle and disappear knowing that one day soon I'll return for my mouse and when I do, I'll finally make him mine. *Every good chase must come to an end.*

***The Past Catches Up**

One Week Ago...

Ever

Hearing the familiar buzz that signals someone being at the front gate, I leave the table and go to the intercom by the door. Pressing the button, I say, "Who is it?"

"I have a delivery for Ever Dracovi."

Looking at the security feed displayed on the screen, I verify that it is indeed a delivery van and say, "Bring it to the house."

I press the button to open the gate and walk over to the door. Opening it, I step out onto the porch and watch the delivery van come up the driveway. The driver parks the van, grabs the package, and gets out. He climbs the stairs and hands me the envelope after scanning it then holds out the scanner to me. "Sign here please."

Seeing the signature line displayed on the scanner's screen, I use the little pen to sign my name.

The driver takes the scanner and says, "Have a nice day," then walks back to his van and drives off.

Once he's through the gates and they close behind him, I tear open the envelope and pull out the contents. Inside is a picture of me and Vincetti from a restaurant we had dinner at last week. There's a red bullseye drawn over Vincetti's face and beside it, also in red, is a poem.

Blood is red

Bruises are blue

I won't let

Him have you.

Fuck. I thought this was over, that he'd given up or died. I really, really hoped he'd died because I hadn't received anything for a while,-not since Cairo when we happened to be on a job in the same city and he sent me dead flowers with more pictures of my dead hook-ups and photoshopped ones of us together plus a note that said he'd claim me soon- but it looks like I was wrong. *Deep down you've known you were wrong for a while.* The curare laced bullet Vincetti was shot with is proof Pieire pulled the trigger. And now, I've put Vincetti square in the bastard's sights. Just when I thought the threat was over, it seems like it's only just begun.

Maybe if I'd considered the possibility that he hadn't contacted me in a while because my new tactics of disappearing as soon as a job is done and moving between safehouses regularly kept him from finding me we wouldn't be in this situation now. I should've rejected Vincetti when we met like I told myself I would twenty years ago but with his life in danger at the time I couldn't bring myself to abandon him like that. *At least if he dies now I'll go with him and this'll finally be over.* There's no way I'm going to let that happen though. I plan to live a long life with Vincetti and Pieire won't be getting in the way of that. *That bastard won't win or get away this time.*

"Is everything alright *Tesoro?*"

I look over my shoulder at Vincetti and smile. "Everything's fine, *moya dusha.*"

Lies...all lies...but I can't tell him there's a new threat. Not yet. He's only just gotten used to not having to look over his shoulder every time he goes out and I refuse to be the one who makes him go back to that. No...I'll take care of this on my own. It's time to face the past instead of running from it.

CHAPTER ONE
THE THREAT IS REAL

Ever

Blood is red

Bruises are blue

I won't let

Him have you.

Rule #10: *If you ever cross paths with a psychopath from your past, kill him.*

Ever since I got that package a week ago, I've had my programs running searches non-stop in an effort to track down Pieire. I've even put every contact I have on the search as well. They're looking for intel through informants and other avenues. I have to find him first and take the fight to him before he does anything to harm Vincetti. The fact that he's the sniper who shot Vincetti and nearly killed him is all the motive I need to take him out. Let's not forget that he's been stalking me for years and all the shit he's done during that time from killing people I'd hooked up with to threatening my family.

I knew the bastard was dangerous the day we met, but at the time I wasn't aware just how dangerous he could be. In fact, I didn't learn it until after we did that job together. The years to follow only served to hammer home the point. Twenty years ago, I decided to come up with a plan to catch and kill Pieire. I knew if everything wasn't perfect there'd be a possibility of Pieire escaping. Which is why, I've spent twenty years doing research and coming up with a number of different plans that I haven't executed yet because I overanalyze every detail. The plan needs to be perfect. It's not worth doing if I fail in the end.

The idea was to make him come to me when I was ready to execute whatever plan I'd settled on and had everything in place. I was close to finally choosing a plan to put into play but meeting Vincetti threw everything off track and now this confrontation is happening a lot sooner than I planned. Nothing I had in mind for this is ready to execute which means I'll be flying by the seat of my pants here and hoping for the best. I'm positive Pieire waited so long to send me something to make me think he'd given up and lull me into a false sense of security. *I fucking fell for it hook line and sinker too.*

Pieire's MO with his gifts hasn't changed at all. The pictures are an intimidation tactic but it won't work this time. I'm going to end this once and for all because I don't want to spend the rest of my and Vincetti's life looking over our shoulders. The time has come to stop running and fight. Over the years I've been running, I've been gathering any intel I possibly can on Pieire in an effort to ensure my plan will be foolproof. *At least, it would've been had I gotten the chance to execute it.*

In an effort to find something I could use against him I've done a ton of research trying to learn everything about him in order to prepare for anything he might do. The first piece of information I uncovered revealed the reason Pieire always calls me little mouse. Pieire is a pit viper shifter and since day one, he's seen me as prey. *He won't be seeing me that way for much longer.* Hell, once I'm done with him, he won't be seeing anything anymore. *But first, I have to find him.*

Pieire is one of the best assassins the council has trained, but I'm better and I know every trick in the book. However, Pieire is smart. For the past twenty years he's always been one step ahead of me and I've never been able to get close to him. If I want to have any kind of chance at taking him out, I'll need to outsmart him, and I know he'll never make it easy. Not when he enjoys watching people suffer and draws it out, so it lasts longer. If someone's suffering was over too quickly, he'd be disappointed. I believe that's why he uses curare laced bullets.

Pieire's perfected the dosage so that the person affected by the poison suffers for hours from it unless they bleed out first, as evidenced by the files in the council database I could pull up on every job he's been on from the time he started until the moment he quit. Like me, he's become a hitman for hire after quitting but he obviously doesn't have the same morals I do when it comes to the kinds of jobs he'll take. Pieire doesn't discriminate. If the money's good, he'll take out women and children, something I'd never do. The man has no sense of remorse or empathy. Hell, any person with an ounce of honor in their body would never harm a woman or child. The fact that Pieire would is proof of how different we are.

Sometimes I wonder what my life would've been like if I'd never joined the council assassins or branched out into solo work after quitting. Every time the thought crosses my mind it's followed by the realization that I probably would've never met Vincetti if I hadn't been an assassin for hire and he'd likely be dead now. Meaning I would've lost out on the chance to ever meet him and make him mine. It's funny how things work but I suppose it's all part of fate's plan. Everything happens for a reason and I believe the path my career has taken is a minor piece on the board game of life fate is playing.

While my searches are running, I go into the kitchen to start breakfast. It's early and Vincetti is still asleep but I've been wide awake since three am because my brain wouldn't shut up. I kept reliving every moment Pieire and I crossed paths. Instead of laying in bed staring at the ceiling letting my mind run wild with scenarios of how Pieire will mount his attack until it was time to get up, I decided perusing any information my searches have turned up so far would be more productive. The downside? I'm still nowhere close to coming up with an answer of where Pieire could be hiding.

I'm definitely better at what I do than he is, but Pieire is cunning and likes to fight dirty. He'll do whatever it takes to get what he wants. *Two can play at this game though.* I've got some of my programs looking for something on Pieire I can use to draw him out of whatever hole he's hiding in. However, I'm not going to hold my breath waiting for it to happen or rely solely on it for my counterattack. Especially, since I haven't found anything of that nature in the years I've been gathering information. Though I suppose he could've buried that kind of info so deep no one would ever come across it easily in an effort to protect someone he cared about like what I've done with my family.

However, I don't see Pieire having any form of emotional ties to anyone. He's cold, soulless, cunning, and ruthless. I doubt he feels anything like love for anyone. Because of the type of man he is I wouldn't put it past him to get rid of anyone or anything that could be used as leverage against him. It won't stop me from trying to find something though. I have to be smart about this and plan accordingly. Even if it means calling in more favors and help. I will find him, it's only a matter of time.

CHAPTER TWO
A MATES FRUSTRATION
Vincetti

Rule #8: If you wake up in bed alone more than three times per week give your mate a talking to.

Waking up to the smell of bacon and coffee, I slip out of bed and head into the bathroom not surprised that Ever isn't in bed with me. This is the fourth time I've woken alone this week. Missing out on a morning romp and cooking breakfast together four days in a row has me frustrated. I can tell Ever has something on his mind but he won't tell me what it is and every time I try to be sneaky and use our mind link to figure it out, he locks up tighter than a vault. I know he'll tell me when he's ready but that doesn't stop me from worrying.

After taking care of business in the bathroom, I pull on a pair of athletic shorts and make my way downstairs. Ever is busy removing the bacon from the pan and putting it on a plate lined with paper towels. Coming up behind him, I wrap my arms around his waist and kiss the back of his neck. "Good morning, *Tesoro*."

Ever turns and kisses me softly. "Good morning, *moya dusha*."

Slipping a finger under the waistband of his sweats, I draw a line back and forth across his belly and say, "It is a good morning, but it would've been a great one if I'd gotten to wake up next to you, have a morning romp between the sheets, and cook breakfast together."

Ever strokes my cheek and says, "I'm sorry, *moya dusha*. I woke up in the middle of the night and couldn't get back to sleep."

"You could've woken me. I'm sure I could've come up with a distraction to tire you out."

Ever barks out a laugh and waggles his eyebrows. "Oh, I'm sure you could've but you looked so peaceful I didn't have the heart to wake you. How about I make you a deal?"

"What kind of deal?"

"As soon as we've eaten, we'll go back upstairs and have that morning romp."

Licking my lips, I say, "I'd love to, *Tesoro,* but I've got an early meeting with my father, so it'll have to be quick and in the shower."

Ever puts our food onto plates and says, "Then let's hurry and eat. If we're quick about it, I can take my time with you in the shower."

"Not too much time though. My father will be furious if I'm late."

Ever winks at me. "Don't worry, *moya dusha,* I'll protect you from his wrath."

"I know you will."

After breakfast and a shower, Ever and I head to pride lands. My father has increased the frequency of his deals. I suppose he wants to make sure everyone is flush with cash before I take over and move into legit business dealings. Father has also taken security to the next level. Not that I blame him. The situation with my uncle and my near-death experience was terrifying for everyone involved. To be honest, Ever and I both have nightmares about it at least once a week. The whole ordeal is going to haunt us for a while. I'm just glad it's over.

While I know I don't have to look over my shoulder anymore, I still find myself being overly cautious. Probably because deep down, I know my uncle won't be the last enemy I face. Some people are bound to be pissed when I take the business legit but that's their problem not mine. I can't in good conscience continue to distribute drugs and guns that'll eventually fall into the hands of children. I don't want to be responsible for supplying something that gets a child killed.

My plan for the business going legit is getting out of guns and drugs and into something more profitable. I've spent every spare moment -when I'm not spending time with Ever or in meetings with my father- putting together a plan for the future. I've decided to open a series of clubs. My plan is to start with two of each, a strip club, a kink club, and a nightclub. One set dedicated solely to paranormals and the other for the general public. If they do well, I'll open more. I also plan to start an escort service providing companions for the rich.

Sex sells but I refuse to let my employees have to rely on the income from prostitution. Will sex be involved in a night with one of my companions? Almost definitely, but that will be a private arrangement between the client and the customer after the initial job is done. My escorts will be paid well for their companion services and the choice to have sex, or not, will always be up to them. But I'll be sure to have policies in place to ensure any sexual acts are done off the clock. Illegal prostitution is not something I want to be involved in. It'll defeat the purpose of taking the business legit.

It's going take a lot of work to get out of the illegal side of things but I'm ready to take on the challenge. I'll have to secure a new pipeline for our distributors with a different family, so I don't piss them off and make more enemies. Once that's done, I can focus solely on getting the clubs up and running. I've been looking at real estate and doing estimates of how much money we could make on average based on the location, expected clientele per night, and sales. If all goes the way I think it will and I expand the way I plan to once the first clubs are doing business, we'll be making almost as much money if not more than we do now.

Ever parks the SUV in front of the main house and we go in together. When we reach my father's office, Ever asks, "Want me to go in with you or wait out here?"

"You can come in with me."

As soon as we enter the office, I sit in one of the empty seats and Ever takes up a position behind my chair. I know it's so he can keep an eye on everyone in the room. My safety is important to him and he works hard to make sure nothing happens to me again. The overprotectiveness can be a bit suffocating at times, but I don't complain because it comes from a good place. Neither of us wants to experience the threat of one of us dying again.

Once the last person arrives the meeting begins. My father says, "We have a new buyer. He's been vouched for by one of our other clients and has placed a large order. However, we've never delivered to his area before which means one of you will need to map out the best route with the least possible risk. Vincetti, who do you think should go?"

Crossing my legs, I rest my clasped hands on my knee and say, "I think you're jumping the gun a bit father. Before we agree to fill this buyer's order, we need to gather intel on him and the client who vouched for him. Just because the new buyer has been vouched for doesn't mean he's trustworthy. For all we know he and the client that vouched for him could be working with the feds. The last thing we need is to be taken down by a federal investigation. Our guys won't survive a human prison."

My father nods and says, "We'll put Guido on it but I believe it would be good idea to get the route mapped out even if we don't fulfill this order because there might be another buyer in the future from that area."

"If that's what you think is best, then I suggest putting Gabriel on it. He's mapped out the last three routes and does a fantastic job."

My father nods and leans back in his chair steepling his fingers. "Alright. Next order of business, I need a few guys to go to the warehouse and take inventory. We need to make sure we have everything needed to fill this new order if the intel on the buyer shows he's not working with the feds. Anything we don't have in stock will be added to the next order from our supplier."

"When is the delivery date?"

"The buyer wants it delivered in four weeks."

Sighing, I run my fingers through my hair and say, "That doesn't give us much time, but we'll make it work. Guido and Gabriel need to get started immediately. We'll give them each a week to get things done. As for the warehouse inventory, that needs to be assessed now. Whoever we assign that task will only get three days to provide us with a list to add to the order. Our next shipment is scheduled to arrive in two weeks, so any last-minute additions need to happen asap."

"We'll get Luigi, Viktor, and Terrance to handle the warehouse."

"Sounds good. What's next on the agenda for today?"

"Progress reports."

I spend the next hour listening to each of my father's men prattle on about how business is doing in each of their assigned territories. After I remind them of what'll happen if they ever sell drugs to kids the meeting is adjourned. On our way out, Ever's phone pings with an alert. He has a special tone assigned to everything so any message or alert that comes through is easily identifiable. This one lets him know that a search program he started is complete.

Seeing the look on his face as he views the alert has me curious. "Is something wrong, *Tesoro?*"

Ever shakes his head and smiles at me but I can tell it's forced. "Everything's fine, *moya dusha.* I have an errand to run. Will you be okay here on your own for a bit?"

Asking him what's going on isn't going to get me any answers. He's determined to keep me out of the loop. While it pisses me off, I understand he just wants to protect me, and I can't fault him for that. Pushing down the anger I feel at him for keeping things from me, I nod. "I'll go visit with my mother while you take care of your errand."

Ever kisses my cheek and says, "I'll try not to be gone too long."

"Okay."

After a kiss goodbye, Ever walks down the hall leaving me with more questions. Something is definitely going on. I know it just like I know he doesn't want to tell me about it. But that's okay. I'm determined to investigate and figure this out on my own. I have to be smart about it though, so he doesn't discover what I'm doing. I have a feeling that whatever he's hiding isn't good and if that's the case then his protective instinct is likely the only reason, he hasn't told me anything. Something I'll be sure to confront him about once whatever danger he's hiding from me has passed.

We're partners and if I'm the target of another psychopath like my uncle then I deserve to know about it. Two heads are better than one when it comes to figuring things out and I know if he'd fill me in on what's going on, we could come up with a solid plan and take care of the threat together. That's not likely to happen though with Ever's protective instincts in overdrive. Right now, Ever doesn't want to risk almost losing me again, so regardless of whether it's a good idea or not he's doing this alone. I can't sit idly by while he puts his life on the line for me again so I'll just have to take matters into my own hands and pray he won't be too upset with me if he ever finds out.

Exiting the pride house, I walk down the path towards my parents' house. Knocking on the door briefly, I enter the house and say, "Mamma are you here?"

Not getting an answer, I search the house for her but come up empty. There's only one other place she could be if she isn't here. Leaving the house, I continue down the path to my aunt's. I've always called her auntie Pix -short for pixie- because she's four foot ten, with wild curly blond hair, is barely a hundred and thirty pounds soaking wet, a total hippie and absolutely looney-tunes. Reminds me of that professor on the *Harry Potter* movies who taught Divination. Still, you can't help but love her. Her front door isn't closed, so instead of knocking, I open the storm door and walk inside. As soon as I step over the threshold, I hear a high-pitched excited squeal of "Vinnie," seconds before my aunt slams into me, wrapping me in a hug.

Hugging her tight, I smile down at her and say, "Hey auntie Pix, it's good to see you."

Auntie Pix lets go of me and loops her arm through mine, leading me towards the patio doors. "Come on, your Mamma is out back in the garden. She's helping me plant my petunias. I came in to get some crystals to put in the garden that'll help things grow."

This woman and her crystals...she has one for everything. Every time I come visit her, she gives me a whole jewelry bag full of crystals that are supposed to help me with whatever happens to be wrong with me whether it's stress or something else. *Hopefully, I can avoid that this time…*I don't need another drawer full of crystals like I used to have in my apartment before it was blown to smithereens.

Once we're outside, Pix says, "Look who came to visit."

Mamma looks up and grins at me. "*Mio figlio,* what a nice surprise. I thought you'd still be in meetings with your father."

"Nope. We're done for the day. I think. He didn't say anything about any other meetings and since Ever had to run an errand I thought I'd visit with you for a little bit. When I didn't find you at home, I knew I'd find you here."

"You know me too well, *mio figlio.*"

Shrugging, I smile and say. "Eh, it's a gift."

She laughs and says, "Would you like to help us plant these flowers?"

"Sure, Mamma."

Kneeling in front of the flowerbed next to her, I put on the pair of gloves Pix hands to me and start planting, letting myself get lost in the repetitiveness of the work.

Ever

Rule #11: *Always assume your enemy is one step ahead of you and plan accordingly.*

After Vincetti's meeting, my computer program got a hit on a credit card registered to one of Pieire's aliases. I know Pieire wouldn't be that careless unless he wanted to be found. *It's probably a trap.* I'm sure he's aware I'm looking for him by now, so this could be an attempt to lure me out. If it is, he's succeeded. But letting him lure me out and falling for an obvious trap are two very different things. The latter of which is never going to happen.

Parking my SUV in front of the seedy motel, I cut the engine and step out. Hitting the lock button on the doors, I go inside. The place is one of those pay by the hour types where prostitutes usually take their johns. Walking up to the front desk, I don't bother to greet the man sitting there flipping through a magazine, instead I search his mind for the information I need. Getting Pieire's room number, I make my way towards the stairs, not trusting that the elevator is in working order. Fate only knows how long it's been since the thing was last inspected.

Finding the correct room number, I'm not surprised to find that the door lock is one you need a regular key to get into instead of a card. Guess whoever owns this shithole decided security wasn't all that important. After picking the lock, I draw the gun I keep in a holster at my back and step into the room. There's no sign of Pieire other than the package that's been left on the bed. Holstering my weapon, I walk over to the bed, keeping an eye out for any possible booby traps.

My sense of smell isn't as good as a wolf's but it's good enough to detect explosives. While I'm sure Pieire wouldn't try to kill me like that -at least not until after he's had his fun- I don't want to take any chances. After scenting the box and determining it doesn't contain a bomb of any kind, I pull my pocket knife out and cut the package open. Inside the box is a snow-globe of the Eiffel tower and a rose with a note attached.

A walk down memory lane

Taped to the snow-globe is an envelope. Opening it, I find a postcard from France with a date and another note. The date corresponds to the moment when Pieire and I crossed paths for the first time since the job we'd done together. The note written on the back of the postcard is another riddle that'll lead me to the next clue.

Well, that's simple enough. I doubt there's many kings who rule without crowns. I just need to figure out *which* king I'm looking for. While I hate that I'll have to play his game if I stand any chance at finding him it has to be done. With any luck my searches will come up with a true lead that wasn't created by Pieire himself and I can end this whole thing without even needing to see this game through to the end. Tearing the notes into tiny pieces, I drop them into the trash with the rose. Returning the snow-globe to the box I tuck it under my arm and exit the motel room. When I walk out of the motel, I see two guys trying to break the window in my SUV using a crowbar. I have to bite back a laugh at them. They're panting heavily and are cursing up a storm.

The guy without the crowbar grabs the arm of the other guy and tries to pull him towards the street. "Let's just go man! We aren't getting in this thing!"

Sneaking up behind them, I say, "That's because the glass is bulletproof." *Glass-clad polycarbonate bulletproof glass for the win.*

They both jump, shout, "Shit!" and take off running. Chuckling, I unlock the doors to the SUV and climb inside. Placing the box on the passenger seat, I start the engine and back out of my parking spot. On the way back to pride lands, I stop by a thrift store and put the snow-globe in their donations bin because Vincetti would have questions if he saw it and I don't want to have to lie about where I got it. It's bad enough that I'm keeping what's going on a secret from him. I refuse to add lying to him on top of that. Lying would break his trust and that's not something I want to do. Keeping secrets to protect him is one thing but lying is a whole other ballgame, one I never plan to play. Faking like everything is okay might technically be lying but a little white lie like that is easily forgivable. A blatant huge lie like the one I'd have to tell if I'd brought that snow-globe home wouldn't be easily forgiven.

When I arrive on pride lands, I drive straight to Vincetti's parents' house. However, the house is empty, so I reach out to Vincetti with our mind link.

Where are you, moya dusha?

At my aunt's house helping her plant flowers. It's the pink house three houses down from my mother's. We're in the backyard.

Leaving the SUV where it is, I walk down the path to the pink house and circle around to the backyard where I find Vincetti, his mother, and the woman who must be his aunt, all kneeling in front of flowerbeds planting flowers. Walking over, I drop to my knees next to Vincetti and greet him with a kiss and a smile.

"Need some help, *moya dusha?*

Vincetti hands me a tray of flowers and says with a grin, "The more the merrier, *Tesoro*. Get to planting."

"Sir, yes, sir."

CHAPTER FOUR
MODERN DAY SHERLOCK HOLMES
Vincetti

Rule #9: Whenever you need to stealthily access your mate's computer system without him knowing, exhaust him with sex first so he sleeps like the dead.

After Ever and I helped finish planting the flowers in aunt Pix's garden we had lunch with her and my mother before returning home. As soon as we got through the door, I attacked Ever like a starved man, catching him by surprise. But he didn't complain. We didn't even make it to the bedroom until round three. The first was in the entryway and the second took place on the stairs.

Right now, Ever is napping and I'm using the opportunity to try and figure out what he's hiding from me while simultaneously preparing dinner so I have an excuse to be out of bed. Ever's laptop is on the counter where he left it, so I don't have to worry about trying to put it back before he wakes up.

Once I have the steaks marinating, I open the laptop and hit the spacebar to take it out of sleep mode. When the password screen pops up, I type in the one he gave me and curse when it comes up as invalid. *Shit...he changed it.* Now, I've got to either attempt to guess it and pray I don't lock him out of his laptop or ask him what the new one is and come up with an excuse as to why I need it.

I don't feel right lying to him so asking might be out of the question. Unless, I come up with a legitimate reason. *I'll try guessing first and if that doesn't work, I'll ask him.* Mamma's birthday is next week, and I already got her a present, but I can always get her another. *One can never have too many presents.* It would be a good explanation if I end up having to ask Ever for the password to his laptop. According to the counter on the screen I have four attempts left. *Let's make them count.*

Typing in my name, I hit enter. When it comes up invalid, I try the date we met which is also the wrong password. *Damn...this is harder than I thought.* There're so many different things it could be

I might never guess. I'll try one more time and if it isn't right, I'll just ask Ever when he wakes up. Staring at the screen, I close my eyes and let my thoughts wander, sorting through all the possibilities when one becomes glaringly obvious. Ever hasn't called me by name since we claimed each other. *Now if I could just figure out how to spell it.*

Pulling out my phone I find a translate website then look up the term of endearment. Armed with the correct spelling of *moya dusha,* I type it into the password screen along with the date we met and hit enter. When it's accepted, I breathe a sigh of relief. *Thank the fates, I got it right.*

Ever has left a search open. It's sorting through tons of information faster than I can read it. He's split the screen so he can view two windows at once. The right side is where the search is running, and the left side is open to a file on a man named Pieire. As I read over everything he has on the man it becomes obvious that he's the assassin who shot me. The search parameters Ever is using tell me he's searching for a location on Pieire. *So, this is what he's been hiding.*

If he's keeping the fact that he's hunting the man who nearly killed me to himself, he must have a good reason. *I wish I knew what the reason was.* Instead of confronting him about it right this minute, I'll keep the fact that I know about what he's doing to myself until the situation is handled even if I don't like that he's hiding things from me. However, as soon as this is taken care of all bets are off. Ever and I haven't really had a big fight since we met but I have a feeling this will be our first. We can't go through life hiding things from each other. That's not how a mating works and I'll be sure to hammer that point home when I confront him. Even if I have to tie him up and deny him orgasms until he swears to never hide things from me again that pertain to our safety and a possible threat to our lives.

Hearing Ever's footsteps on the stairs, I minimize his windows then open the internet and type in a shopping website, so he doesn't realize I was snooping. Jumping over to the women's jewelry section, I start scrolling through the options. Ever comes up behind me and kisses the back of my neck then wraps his arms around my waist and rests his chin on my shoulder. "What are you looking at, *moya dusha?*"

"Jewelry. I was thinking of getting something else for Mamma's birthday present."

He points to a rose gold bracelet with diamonds and a heart charm that can be engraved and has the option of adding one or multiple birthstones. "I think she'd like that. We can pay extra for shipping to make sure it's here on time."

Wiggling in my seat excitedly, I say, "Great! I'll order one. By the way, *Tesoro,* why didn't you tell me you changed your password?"

"Sorry, *moya dusha,* I meant to tell you, it just slipped my mind. I change all my passwords every three months to make it harder for hackers to get into my system," then with a chuckle he says, "But it seems you figured it out."

Looking over my shoulder at him, I wink and say, "If I didn't know you, I would've never guessed it. It took me four tries before I finally got it right."

Ever laughs and says, "Good thing it didn't take five otherwise my self-destruct program would've wiped everything from the laptop and fry the hard drive."

My mouth drops open in shock. "Seriously? I thought it would only lock you out of the account for a little while."

Ever shakes his head. "Nope. I'm a paranoid bastard, *moya dusha.* On the off chance anyone ever gets their hands on my computer, I want it to be impossible for them to get any important information from it."

Nodding, I say, "That makes sense, *Tesoro.* With the job you do I'm sure you've made enemies."

A strange look I can't decipher crosses his face before he can mask it and has me wondering if there's more to the situation than what I found. "I have but only a few have ever been able to track me down. Still, it pays to be overly cautious because the minute I drop my guard an enemy can strike. Which could be fatal for both of us and I refuse to take that risk."

Turning on the stool until I'm facing him, I wrap my arms around him and say, "I understand, *Tesoro*. I wouldn't want you to take that risk either. Nearly dying once was enough. I have no desire to repeat that experience."

Ever kisses the top of my head and says, "Neither do I, *moya dusha*."

Sitting back, I smile at him. "Okay, enough heavy stuff. Let's get Mamma's present ordered and then we can finish dinner. I've got steaks marinating."

Ever kisses me softly and says, "I'll go fire up the grill so it can heat up."

When he walks out the patio doors, I turn back to the computer and start personalizing Mamma's gift. As soon as I have it ordered, I put his laptop into sleep mode and get to work on the side dishes for dinner. Ever comes in and grabs the steaks then goes back outside. When I finish chopping the veggies and potatoes for the foil packets that'll go on the grill, I season them and drop a few dollops of butter in then seal the packets. Placing the packets on a plate, I walk out onto the patio. Instead of walking right to Ever, I take a moment to admire how sexy he is wearing nothing but a pair of sweatpants. Seeing all that inked skin on display as I let my gaze travel over his body has me hungry for him all over again. But right now, our empty stomachs take precedence. If we wait any longer to eat something my stomach is liable to devour itself. The noises it's been making attest to that fact.

Ever's voice is teasing when he asks, "Like what you see, *moya dusha?*"

Lifting my gaze from his ass, I see he's watching me with a raised eyebrow and a smirk, eyes dancing with mirth. Grinning I wink at him and say, "You know I do, *Tesoro*. After dinner, I'll show you just how much I like the view. All night long."

Ever winks at me and says, "You'd better deliver on that promise, *moya dusha*."

Waggling my eyebrows, I say, "Oh, I will *Tesoro*. Trust me."

Ever

Rule #12: *Whenever you need a distraction to take your mind off things let your mate be it.*

After hours of mind-blowing orgasms, I'm surprisingly still wide awake. Vincetti is sound asleep and it's almost two in the morning. Not willing to lay in bed and stare at the ceiling any longer I go downstairs to check my computer. I can't believe Vincetti managed to guess the password. I'll have to be more careful if I want to keep him from finding out about Pieire. I have a feeling he might already know since I distinctly remember leaving my search windows open when I put my laptop in sleep mode. *He hasn't said anything though which could mean*

I'm not looking forward to finding out the answer. Either option spells trouble in the form of my mate being pissed at me for hiding things. However, saving his life is worth any anger he sends my way. Waking up my laptop when I get into the kitchen, I open the window to my program that is still running the search but hasn't turned up anything useful so far. My only choice for now is to solve the riddle Pieire left for me.

After an hour of poring over a list of anything in Georgia with reference to kings I've narrowed down the possible clue locations to two options. Either the riddle is referring to Elvis Presley or it's referring to the king of the jungle. Since there isn't a landmark or anything nearby that has to do with Elvis, I'm leaning more towards the king of the jungle as the answer. Which is why, I'm currently breaking into the local zoo. I hacked into their security feed and put the footage on a loop so I could walk around freely. I'll return it to normal once I'm gone. I just hope I'm right about the clue location otherwise I'll likely be heading out of state to search for the clue at a location pertaining to Elvis. *Explaining a trip like that without lying about where I'm going would be next to impossible.*

Following the map of the zoo I head for the Africa section where the lion exhibit is located. When I get to the Africa section, I let another map direct me to where the lions are. Jumping over the railing into the enclosure I do my best to land as quietly as possible. I may not see the lions from where I am but that doesn't mean they aren't around. I should've done some research before I left so I'd know if this zoo lets their animals stay on exhibit at night instead of bringing them in.

While I really have nothing to worry about since the lions will see me as a predator and won't attack me it still helps to be cautious. Using the flashlight on my phone I walk through the exhibit looking for the clue. Not finding anything on the ground or in the few trees littering the place I decide to check the rocks. They're the only place left where the clue could be. *Unless Pieire decided to put it on a collar around a lion's neck.* Yeah...that wouldn't be good.

Climbing up onto the rock formation in the center of the exhibit I freeze when I see the lions sleeping there. Spotting the clue dead center in front of them I sigh and sneak over as slow and quiet as possible. Grabbing the miniature replica of the colosseum I turn and use my increased speed to get away quick and run up the wall to get out of the exhibit. I could've left via the door the staff use but since I don't know my way around the behind-the-scenes section of this place that would've been a bad idea. The last thing I need is to get lost in there or set off some kind of hidden alarm.

Leaving the zoo, I walk over to where I parked my SUV. Once I climb inside, I turn on the overhead lights and search the replica for the note. Not finding it inside I flip the replica over and again find nothing. Growling in frustration, I toss the replica into the passenger seat where it bumps the door. Hearing a click like a button being depressed I look over at the replica and see a post card of Rome rising from the floor of it. Taking the card, I flip it over and read the note on the back.

You've found the king

Now onto the next thing

The river's mouth you seek

Is at the bear's feet

*Well this makes no sense at all...*Starting the engine, I pull out of the parking lot. Stopping at another donation bin, I drop the colosseum replica in it and the clue in the trash since I have it memorized now. Once that's done, I grab my tablet and fix the zoo's security feed before getting back on the road and heading home. I don't want Vincetti to wake up and realize I'm gone. I'll have to work out what the riddle means another time. Though if past clues are any indication, I'm sure the riddle pertains to a place we met in the past. With that thought comes the realization that I know exactly what the riddle means. It makes sense now. *Gods I'm an idiot.*

Turning the SUV around I head towards the only Irish pub nearby called The Bearfoot. They have a giant bear statue right out front so even though the place is closed I should be able to find the clue there. *Unless Pieire hid it inside then I'll have to break in.* I'm hoping he didn't. I've had enough breaking and entering for one night.

Before I reach the pub, I turn on the signal jammer, so the security feeds are scrambled when I park in the lot at The Bearfoot and hop out. Strolling over to the bear statue. Sitting at its feet is a bottle of expensive Irish whiskey with a note attached to the neck. *I think I might keep this one...after I make sure it's not poisoned or anything.* Good Irish whiskey isn't something I'll throw in the trash or dump down the drain even if it is from someone I despise with every fiber of my being.

Walking back to my SUV, I climb inside, turn on the overhead light again, and pull the note from the bottle. Opening the card, I read the next clue.

Our journey's almost done

But getting there has been fun.

To locate me

Find Re

Find Re...*Fuck*...There's only one place I know of that has Re in the name and it no longer exists. The land is still there though so maybe I'll find something. The problem is this clue means an hour and a half long road trip when traffic is light. Longer if it isn't. So, if I want to find the next clue, I'll have to come clean Vincetti. *Or I can take a guess at where this is all heading and prepare for it.* I'll worry about the details later though. Ripping the note to shreds I toss it in the little trash can I keep hanging on the back of the seat. I pull out of the parking lot then turn towards home and pray Vincetti is still asleep by the time I get back.

On the drive home, I come up with a plan. I have a feeling I know where Pieire is going with this. If I'm right and set this up correctly this'll all be over soon. Pulling into the garage at the house twenty-minutes later, I send a text to an old friend officially putting my new plan into motion before heading inside where I rejoin a sleeping Vincetti.

CHAPTER SIX
A CHANGE OF PLANS
Vincetti

Rule #10: *Whenever possible wake your sleeping mate with a blowjob.*

I wake up before Ever does. Not surprising since he left in the middle of the night for some reason. I assume it has something to do with Pieire. I just wish he'd talk to me about it. I'm starting to feel like he doesn't trust me even though I know he does. I understand his motives but that doesn't make it hurt any less. Raising up on an elbow, I rest my head in my hand and watch him sleep. When he left last night, I considered following him but decided against it. I might not feel like he trusts me right now, but I trust him and knowing he's doing this to protect me means I'm not about to take unnecessary risks and put myself in danger.

While I want to believe that Pieire isn't after me anymore since my uncle is dead and he won't get paid for killing me I know there's a chance he'd come after me if he figures out Ever is hunting him on my behalf. If he hasn't already figured it out. Realization dawns and I curse to myself. *Fuck...what if that's exactly the reason Ever is hunting him?* If he's still after me of course Ever would want to get to him first before he can make an attempt on my life again. *I should've known this wouldn't end with my uncle's death like I foolishly thought.* I let my guard down thinking we'd taken care of the enemy but obviously Ever hadn't and now he's fighting this battle alone refusing to put me at risk. His protectiveness would be adorable if it wasn't so frustrating. I don't like being treated like a damsel in distress. *Waiting to have this talk isn't an option anymore now that he's sneaking out of the house in the middle of the night to go do who knows what.*

If we weren't fated mates and bonded and had no idea what was going on, I'd think he had a lover on the side he was sneaking out to see. Since I do know, I think it's time to let him in on that little secret. I don't care if he's pissed at me for snooping. This is my life we're talking about and I deserve to know when it's being threatened.

Sighing, I shake off the anger. I'm not going to let it darken my mood this early in the morning. If I do it'll ruin my plans for the day. I don't have any meetings today so I'm hoping Ever and I can spend it together. I don't care what we do though I'm hoping for an outing of some kind. *I'll understand if that isn't an option.* We'll have to talk about things before going anywhere but first I think I'll enjoy a normal morning with Ever.

Smiling to myself, I slip under the sheet and move between Ever's legs. I press gentle kisses to his inner thigh from knee to hip on one leg then repeat the process on the other before zeroing in on my main target. Laving each of his balls with my tongue briefly I then lick my way up the shaft of his hard cock and take it into my mouth. *I do so love morning wood...makes waking him like this easy.*

Circling the tip with my tongue I tease his slit enjoying the taste of his pre-come. Ever lets out a soft moan and shifts his hips. He's not awake yet but he will be soon enough. I continue to tease him until his moans become more frequent and his hands find their way into my hair. Grinning when he begins thrusting his hips, I swallow him to the root and suck hard pulling a moaned, "Fuck yes," from him.

One hand leaves my hair and a moment later Ever is tapping my shoulder with a bottle of lube. Taking it from him, I squirt some on my fingers and toss the bottle aside. Circling his hole with one finger I push it into him spreading the lube around. Knowing he likes the burn I quickly insert a second finger and scissor them. When I brush over his prostate, Ever thrusts hard and groans as he comes. Swallowing every drop, I slip a third finger into him while continuing to suck his cock, so he stays hard.

As soon as he's prepped enough, I let his cock fall from my lips and kiss my way up his body. Positioning myself, I thrust inside him stopping once he's taken all of me to give him a chance to adjust.

Ever moans, "Move, *moya dusha*," then wraps his arms and legs around me.

Grinning at him, I say, "Sure thing, bossy," and begin to move in and out of him. Leaning down, I take his mouth in a slow, explorative kiss keeping with the steady pace of my thrusts. One of Ever's fangs scrapes my tongue and I moan into his mouth at the zing of arousal one little scratch shoots through me. Increasing my pace, I pull away from him in favor of kissing and nibbling my way down his neck. When I gently nip the scar of his claiming bite, Ever groans and his nails dig into my back but he doesn't come. I can tell he's close though and it's taking all of his willpower not to let go so soon.

Sliding my hands down his arms, I grip his wrists and pull his hands away from my back. Linking our fingers together, I pin his arms above his head and grin down at him as I thrust into him hard and peg his prostate. The move has him arching his back and groaning, "Yes, *moya dusha*. Give it to me."

Continuing to peg his prostate with each hard thrust, I feel my animal half rise to the surface ready to claim Ever again. Our bond is already sealed but I love getting off on his bite as much as he loves getting off on mine, so we continue to do it every chance we get. Licking my lips, I smile down at Ever whose eyes have turned red with his arousal. When he tilts his head to the side in invitation, I strike, sinking my shifted canines into his neck.

Ever's loud moan is quickly followed by the scent of his come as his release coats our chests and bellies. Removing my teeth, I seal the wound in his neck. Before I can move away, the sting of Ever's bite floods my body with arousal that sends me over the edge as he drinks my blood. Each sucking pull on my neck is like a line straight to my cock that draws out my orgasm. Moaning, I tangle my fingers in Ever's hair holding him to me until he's finished.

Ever seals the wound in my neck and practically purrs, "Now that, is the best way to wake up."

Kissing his forehead I say, "I'm glad you thought so, *Tesoro*. Maybe now you'll stay in bed even if you can't sleep."

Ever grins and winks. "I think you've persuaded me."

Kissing him softly, I move off him and say, "Good. How about we go downstairs and fix breakfast? I'm thinking cinnamon roll pancakes with bacon and sausage."

"Sounds good, *moya dusha* but I think we should clean-up first. Care to join me for a shower?"

"I have a better idea." Grinning wickedly, I reach into the nightstand drawer and pull out a butt plug then grab a few wet wipes from the jar next to the lamp.

Ever chuckles and says, "I like the way you think, *moya dusha*," then takes some of the wipes and uses them to clean himself up. I use the remaining wipes on myself then slip the plug inside him making him moan. Seeing his cock start to fill with arousal I move off the bed and grab a pair of athletic shorts pulling them on. "Breakfast first, round two later."

Ever stands and stretches then pulls on a pair of pajama pants. With a raised eyebrow he asks, "Is this what I have to look forward to today?"

Playing innocent, I tilt my head to the side and act like I have no idea what he's talking about. "What do you mean?"

Ever laughs his eyes sparkling with amusement. "You know exactly what I mean."

Winking at him, I say, "Guess you'll have to wait and see," and head downstairs.

While I get the pans needed for cooking breakfast, Ever grabs the ingredients. Once I have the bacon and sausage started, I put on a pot of coffee. Ever whips up the batter for the pancakes and starts cooking them. *After we eat, we'll talk.* The last thing I want is for us to argue but we can't move forward with our relationship without addressing this issue. Sighing, I focus on finishing the bacon and sausage then pour us both a cup of coffee.

As soon as everything is finished, we carry everything over to the table and dig in. We're halfway through our meal when Ever puts his fork down and says, "Okay, what's wrong, *moya dusha?* You haven't said a word since we came downstairs and you've been sighing intermittently since the moment you started cooking until now."

Dropping my fork onto my plate, I sigh and push it aside. "I was hoping we'd finish eating before I had to bring this up."

Ever reaches across the table and takes my hand in his. "Tell me what's on your mind, *moya dusha.*"

"I know about Pieire. You'd been acting strange and shutting me out, so I wanted to know why. I saw your program when I cracked the password on your laptop and after reading the information you had, I knew you were hunting him."

Ever pulls his hand from mine and says, "So you lied about why you were on my laptop?"

"Buying Mamma another gift was just an excuse for if you caught me. Which you did. I didn't lie, I just didn't tell you the real reason."

"A lie by omission is still a lie, Vincetti."

The use of my name stings. He hasn't called me by name since he started calling me *moya dusha*. It tells me how angry he is but he's not the only one who gets to be that way. Growling, I say, "Pot meet kettle. You've kept what you've been doing hidden from me. We're mates. Mates are supposed to communicate. You don't get to shut me out because you think you're protecting me. I get you want Pieire to pay for what he did to me, but you could've told me. Keeping things from me and lying to me about everything being fine is not what a relationship should be built on."

Ever stands -his chair flying back and crashing to the floor with the force of his movements- and shouts, "Of course I want him to pay, but that's not why I've kept this from you! I don't want you to be looking over your shoulder and worrying if today will be the day he attacks."

"I already look over my shoulder! It comes with the territory of being a mob boss's son! My uncle was proof of that! Besides, how do you know Pieire will attack? It's not like he'll be getting paid anymore since my uncle is dead."

Ever roughly jerks his fingers through his hair looking utterly defeated when he says, "He has a bigger motivation than money."

Crossing my arms, I raise an eyebrow and ask, "What motivation is that?"

"Me."

Shock doesn't even begin to cover what I'm feeling right now. That was not the response I expected. "You? Why would you be his motivation?"

Ever picks up his chair and collapses into it burying his head in his hands. "Pieire has been stalking me ever since we did a job together thirty-five years ago. He's a psychopathic lunatic that's completely obsessed with making me his. When we met, I hadn't heard from him in fifteen years and I stupidly thought he'd died or given up. Your uncle brought him here, but I put you on his radar." Before I can say anything Ever raises his head and the cold expression on his face isn't one I've seen before. "I'm hunting Pieire because if I don't find him and stop him before he has the chance to get to you, we're both dead and I can assure you, it won't be quick."

Circling around the table, I crawl into his lap and wrap my arms around him. "You should've told me, *Tesoro*."

Ever nods. "I know. I'm sorry. I was only thinking of keeping you safe."

Letting my fingers brush through his hair, I say, "I know and I love you for that, but I'm not a damsel in distress and I don't like you going off alone without me knowing the situation. If you'd found him and gotten yourself killed then keeping me safe would be a moot point. We're a team. By keeping me in the loop and letting me help you we can keep each other safe. And if one or both of us dies, then at least we'll have died together."

Ever sighs and smiles faintly. "You and your logic. I swear, from here on out I'll keep you in the loop and will no longer hide things from you."

"That's all I ask, *Tesoro*. Now, tell me everything and don't leave out a single detail."

Ever raises an eyebrow at me and asks, "Where should I start?"

"The beginning."

CHAPTER SEVEN
it's all coming together
Ever

Rule #13: *Make up sex after an argument is always mandatory.*

"So, what's the plan?"

Looking down at a bleary-eyed Vincetti -who's been draped across my chest asleep for the past few hours after we had another morning romp when we'd finished discussing Pieire- and say, "I called an old friend. He's someone I worked with while I was employed by the council and will be here sometime today. Since there are a couple places where the final showdown will happen, we'll come up with a plan for each."

Winking at him I add, "I'd planned to tell you everything before he got here because there was no way I could keep this hidden from you any longer.

Not with you likely wanting to know who he was and why he'd suddenly shown up on top of needing to go over an hour away to find a clue. You and your detective skills just beat me to it. Maybe I should start calling you Sherlock."

Vincetti smacks my chest lightly and says, "Don't you dare, smartass," then his expression turns confusingly thoughtful when he questions, "Wait, you're bringing in the council on this?"

I nod.

"Why?"

Grinning maniacally, I say, "Pierre has been wanted by the council for years ever since he completed a contract on a council member and his entire family and didn't bother to hide that he was the one to do it. If I killed him and the council found out I'd known he was here and didn't report it, I'd be going to Prison."

"Won't they send in a whole bunch of people to hunt him down?"

I shake my head. "No. For two reasons. The first, they don't want to tip him off and have him disappear before they can catch him again. The second, by calling my friend instead of the council as a whole I've ensured he and his small team are the only ones on the case."

Vincetti asks, "How can he do that?"

"He's the team leader for the council's Execution Squad. Pieire's actions are a death sentence so calling that team in on a wanted criminal automatically makes this a sanctioned hit. It doesn't matter who carries it out whether it's me or my friend's guys as long as the end result is the same. Doing things this way means the kill will be justified and I won't end up in jail even if Pieire is unarmed when it happens."

"Because it was council ordered?"

"Exactly."

"Where are the possible locations?"

Brushing my fingers over his back I say, "The old council headquarters where we first met and where we did the first job."

Vincetti tilts his head to the side and asks, "You don't think it'll be anywhere local like where he sent you to find the clues?"

"It's possible, but I doubt it. I've already done the research based on the other clues. There's nothing local that could be associated with those two places. I won't know for sure until I go retrieve the last clue. It's an hour and a half's drive away if traffic isn't bad so I'll go after a plan is formed."

Vincetti leans up on his elbow and asks, "Want me to come with you?"

Before I can answer his phone starts ringing. Putting a finger to my lips, Vincetti winks and says, "Hold that thought," then rolls away to grab his phone from the nightstand on his side of the bed.

When he answers the call with, "Hello father," I have a feeling our plans for the rest of the day before Judge and his team arrive are about to change. No one knows the team's real names just their code names which all have some sort of court reference. There's Judge, Jury, Law, Justice, and Bail.

Vincetti's yelled, "What do you mean he moved up the delivery date," from across the room where he's pacing pulls my attention to him. "You told him what? Why would you tell him we had everything when he hasn't been properly vetted yet? Is the route even plotted?"

Vincetti pinches the bridge of his nose and growls, "You're a stupid old fool and if we go down because of this it's on your head because your greedy ass wouldn't listen to reason. I'll accompany the shipment myself to make sure things go smoothly. Goodbye father."

Vincetti stabs the end call button harder than is necessary and growls, "Stupid old man. If he weren't my mother's fated mate I'd kill him."

"What's going on, *moya dusha?*"

Vincetti stomps over to the closet and grabs one of his suits off a hanger so forcefully I'm surprised he didn't rip the fabric. "My father is what's wrong. We have a new buyer that another client vouched for but being the stubborn bastard he is he refuses to think of the risks. He told the buyer we'd do the delivery since we already have what the buyer has asked for in stock and it isn't set to go to anyone else. As a result, the buyer moved up the delivery date from four weeks from now to tonight. Since my father didn't wait for the vetting process to finish, we have no idea who we're dealing with. If the buyer turns out to be a fed we're fucked."

Standing, I walk over to him and wrap my arms around his waist. He sighs and relaxes against me. "I'm sorry, *Tesoro,* I won't be able to go with you when you retrieve that clue since I have to accompany the shipment."

Turning him to face me I say, "You aren't going alone. I can retrieve the clue another time. I'll go with you tonight."

Vincetti shakes his head but before he can say anything the security alert on my phone dings. Walking over to the nightstand I grab it and see that there's a black SUV sitting at the front gates. The driver side window is rolled down revealing Judge behind the wheel. Pressing the button on my security app to let them through I go into the closet and put on a pair of jeans and a t-shirt then return to the bedroom where Vincetti is pulling on his dress shoes. "Judge and his men are here. I'm going downstairs to let them in, but we aren't done talking."

Kissing his forehead, I walk downstairs reaching the door just in time for the bell to ring. Opening it, I lift my chin and say, "Judge, thanks for coming," then step aside to let him and the other guys in.

Judge takes my hand and pulls me into a one-armed back slapping hug. With a smile he says, "Good to see you Ever. Where can we set up?"

"Kitchen's fine."

Vincetti comes down the stairs and heads for the door leading into the garage. "*Moya dusha* wait!"

Vincetti turns and says, "I can't, *Tesoro*. I've got to get to the warehouse and oversee the loading of the shipment before transport."

"I'll come with you."

Vincetti shakes his head. "No. You have to stay here and come up with a plan to take down Pieire. I'll be fine."

"I don't trust your father's men to keep you safe. Get someone else to cover overseeing loading the shipment so I can accompany you on the delivery. Please, *moya dusha*.”

Vincetti crosses the room and takes my face between his hands. “I’ll be okay, *Tesoro*. You’re needed here and we don’t actually know how long planning would take. Waiting just isn’t feasible, I’m sorry.”

Sighing, I nod. “I don’t like it, but I get it. At least take my SUV so I can have peace of mind that no one will get to you on your way to the warehouse and the delivery location. I’d suggest you staying inside it while you oversaw the loading process and delivery, but I know that’s not something you’d do.”

Vincetti chuckles. “You’d be right, but I swear to you I’ll be careful. Plus, we have a mind link so if something goes wrong, you’ll know. I’ll check in with you through it every fifteen minutes.”

Grinning, I hug him tight and kiss him softly. “I’ll hold you to that.”

Feeling a presence behind me I look over my shoulder and see Judge holding out something to me. Taking it from him I realize it’s the tiniest GPS tracker I’ve ever seen. Nodding my thanks to Judge, I slip the tracker under the collar of Vincetti’s button down shirt in the back and kiss him again. Vincetti steps away from me and says, “I’ll be back soon.”

“You’d better.”

He turns on his heel and heads for the garage. As I watch him walk away a pit of dread begins to form in my stomach and I pray I didn't just make a huge mistake.

Turning to face Judge and his men, I walk over to the kitchen island where I left my laptop and say, "Let's get to work."

CHAPTER EIGHT
AMBUSH
Vincetti

Rule #11: *When your mate wants to accompany you everywhere during a dangerous situation...let him.*

Why did I convince Ever he didn't need to come along? Answer, because I'm an idiot who thought his plan was more important than coming with me on what was supposed to be a routine delivery. *I should've listened to him*. If I had maybe I wouldn't be in this situation right now.

After overseeing the loading of the shipment, myself and some of my father's men tasked with transport drove three hours away to the drop off location which turned out to be an abandoned airfield. Standing in front of a private plane waiting on the tarmac was a lone man, no guards in sight. Though that didn't mean they weren't around. I'd been on enough deliveries to know that some buyers keep their security out of sight. But even then, they usually have one or two at their sides which made this situation seem odd.

Chalking my concerns up to paranoia was a mistake. As soon as the other guys and I exited our vehicles the man standing by the plane drew two guns and killed each of the men before they could react. When the man stepped out of the shadows of the plane and said, "Hello, Vincetti," I knew I was in deep shit. A point proven when he raised another gun and fired it at me. Instead of a bullet, I was hit with a dart and I barely had enough time to contact Ever through our mind link with the word ambush before my world went black.

Now, I'm wide awake and stuck inside what I'm sure is a coffin judging by the padding surrounding me. Quite fitting since I'm sure I'm on my way to meet my execution. *Stop being morbid V. Ever will get you out of this mess and then you can apologize for being so stupid.* Thinking of Ever, I try to contact him through our mind link, but it doesn't work. There must've been something in whatever drug Pieire dosed me that is affecting my link with Ever because my connection to him is muted as is my connection to my animal half. *Pieire probably put something in the drug that'll prevent me from shifting only it's working on the mind link too.* Hearing a hiss as air is pumped into the coffin, I sigh with relief knowing I won't suffocate. That relief is short lived because I start feeling groggy again.

When I wake the second time, I'm bound to a chair and gagged. The chair is bolted to the concrete floor and I'm surrounded by the remnants of a building that's been burnt down. Pieire is sitting in a chair across from me his attention on the phone in his hand. The twisted smile on his face sends shivers down my spine and not the good kind either. Pieire looks up from his phone and says, "You're awake...that won't do." Pulling a syringe from his pocket, Pieire walks over to me and pulls my collar down to expose the side of my neck. The expression on his face turns malicious and I know he's seen the mark on my neck. Pieire growls but instead of losing control he jabs the needle into my neck, depressing the plunger. "I need you to sleep for a few more hours. When Ever arrives the real fun can begin."

As soon as my eyes start to droop, Pieire smirks and pats my cheek. The last thing I hear is his whispered, "I'm going to enjoy tearing you apart while he watches," before the darkness drags me under.

The next time I wake it's to water being thrown in my face. Pieire's grin is evil when he says, "Wakey-wakey, we've got company." He moves behind my chair and presses a gun to the back of my head as a high-speed blur skids to a stop in front of us. Ever's face is a cold blank mask but his eyes reveal how pissed he is. "Pieire, let Vincetti go. This is between you and me."

Pieire says, "No can do, little mouse. It stopped being between you and me a long time ago."

Pieire presses the gun to the back of my head harder really digging in with it making me wince. Ever's eyes narrow and his hands clench into fists with barely controlled rage. "Let. Him. Go. Now."

"No. He's going to pay for touching what's mine and you're going to watch."

Ever's cool façade shatters and he shouts, "Like hell I am. You harm him and I'll kill you. It won't be quick either. I'll ensure that you suffer."

Pieire shouts, "I'm already suffering," and the gun moves away from my head. Tilting my head back, I see he's waving the gun around as he begins to rant. "You're mine not his! Not anyone else's! Mine! No one is supposed to touch you and you aren't supposed to touch anyone who isn't me. That's how mating works yet you keep choosing other people over me. For years, I've watched and waited.

Sent you gifts and took out the competition so you'd realize we belong together and choose me like fate intended. But. You. Never. Did," he grits out that last part through clenched teeth.

As if to hammer home a point, Pieire grips the collar of my shirt and rips it away shouting, "To make matters worse, you bonded with this one. It should've been me you bastard and you're going to pay for your mistake starting with watching me end this interloper's life. Once he's gone then we can be happy together. You'll see."

Holy shit...he's completely off his rocker. As much as I wish Ever would just do something, I know he's got a plan and I can't exactly voice my desire for him to end this bullshit with the gag in my mouth. Not only that, if he acts rashly it could mean our deaths so even though I hate that he's just standing there I know it's for the best so I force myself to be patient and let this play out. *It'll all be over soon. I know it.*

Ever says, "We aren't mates Pieire and I'm not yours. I never will be. My heart belongs to the man you have tied to that chair and if you kill him, I'll die too."

Pieire snarls, "Then you'll die because if I can't have you no one can," and turns the gun on Ever. Before he can pull the trigger, the loud rapport of a gunshot is heard in the distance and is quickly followed by the sound of flesh hitting the unforgiving concrete behind me. In a flash, Ever is cutting me free and pulling me into his arms. "*Moya dusha,* thank the gods you're alright."

Wrapping my arms around him, I bury my face in his neck taking in his scent and sigh. "I'm sorry for being so stupid, *Tesoro.* I never should've talked you into staying behind."

"Hush, *moya dusha.* There's no need to apologize. You were right. I needed to stay behind and come up with a plan." With a shrug, he continues, "Besides, I'm the one who should've realized that a new buyer suddenly popping up when your dad hasn't accepted new clients in a year was completely suspicious. It's obvious this was a trap and the only reason it worked is because you went on your own. If I'd been there, Pieire might not have made a move. I have no doubt he was surveilling you from the moment you left the house and would know if I were with you or not."

Looking over my shoulder at where Pieire fell, I see the hole between his eyes and the blood pooling around him. Turning back to Ever I say, "I feel like it shouldn't have been this easy."

Ever nods in agreement. "It shouldn't have been but in his arrogance at thinking he had us exactly where he wanted us, he got sloppy. Instead of setting traps to be sure anyone I might've brought with me couldn't get the drop on him he was more interested in making us both suffer."

Judge comes up behind Ever with a large rifle strapped to his back and says, "We'll take over from here. There's a plane waiting for you at a private airstrip twenty miles from here. Have a safe trip home." *Fuck, I have so many questions.*

Ever shakes Judge's hand and says, "Thanks for the help man, I owe you one."

Judge grins and says, "I'll cash in that favor sometime," patting Ever on the back before walking away to make a call.

Taking that as a dismissal Ever leads me from the building letting me lean against him since whatever drugs are left in my system are making it hard to walk on my own and are still keeping my link to him and my animal half muted. After I stumble for the second time Ever sweeps me into his arms bridal style and takes off running until we reach a vehicle parked in between a set of trees. He carefully places me in the passenger seat and circles around to the driver side.

Once we're on the road, I lose all control of my mouth and start firing off questions. "How did you know where I was? Did you have time to find the last clue? Where are the rest of Judge's team? For that matter, where are we?"

Ever laughs and says, "Easy there, speedy. Give me a chance to answer before you ask another question."

Blushing, I say, "Sorry, I couldn't hold back the questions anymore."

"To answer your questions, I didn't have time to find the last clue. I only knew where you were because Pieire sent a picture of you bound and gagged with the message 'You didn't find Re but that's okay. Here's a message from a friend. The beginning is the end.' That combined with the picture and the tracker I slipped under your collar before you left made figuring out where you were easy." *A tracker huh? Smart man.*

He takes my hand in his and squeezes it before continuing, "The remnants of the building you were in was once the council headquarters before the building caught fire and the council moved to a new location. Where we are is in upstate New York. We have a two-and-a-half-hour flight ahead of us. Judge's men were spread out around the woods. Whoever had the best shot at Pieire took it."

Nodding, I say, "I see. Why didn't they show up with Judge though?"

"Their job is to make sure Pieire didn't plan for back up to arrive while also ensuring that we get home safely. Once we're clear, they'll dispose of Pieire's body and file a report with the council."

"So just like that it's over?"

Ever nods. "For now."

Raising an eyebrow, I ask, "Why do you say, 'for now'?"

"Because after what's happened, I have no doubts that there'll be another enemy in the future. Between my past and you taking your father's business legit someone is bound to pop up wanting to kill us."

Squeezing his hand, I say, "If it does happen, we'll fight them together. No more hiding things or doing things alone. We're stronger with each other than we are apart."

"Yes, we are."

Leaning over the center console, I kiss his cheek and say, "Now, let's go home. I'm in need of a long hot soak in the bathtub, a hot meal, you, and a bed."

Ever grins and says, "Your wish is my command, *moya dusha,*" then pushes the accelerator all the way to the floor speeding to the airstrip where we'll find our ride home.

CHAPTER NINE
THE CALM AFTER THE STORM
Ever

Two days later...

Rule #14: *Always sew a tracker into every new piece of clothing your mate buys *even if they're for you* on the off chance he gets kidnapped again and vice versa. *Note to self: Teach Vincetti how to use tracking program in case you're the one who gets kidnapped next time.**

Rule #15: *Next time you invite your family for a visit give your mate some warning.*

Exiting the shower, I grab a towel and wrap it around my waist. Vincetti was supposed to join me but instead he went downstairs to wait for his father to arrive. As soon as we got back from New York Vincetti called his father and ripped him a new one for not waiting for the vetting process to complete. Vincetti didn't want to see the man anytime soon but his mother convinced him to. *Speaking of mothers, I wonder what time it is...*I called my mother to let her know she and my sister didn't have to run anymore and gave her the address to the house so they could come visit. I didn't expect them to hop on a plane immediately. They're supposed to arrive by noon.

Walking into the bedroom, I head into the closet to dress. I've just pulled my shirt on when Vincetti comes up behind me and wraps his arms around my waist. He nips my ear and growls sexily, "You know, a little warning would've been nice."

"Warning about what?"

"Your family dropping in for a visit. I thought the SUV I buzzed through the gates was my father but turns out it was an Uber dropping off your mom and sister. They're downstairs."

Turning to face him, I give him my best innocent smile and say, "Surprise?"

He narrows his eyes at me, and I laugh. "I was going to tell you last night when I got the message that they were hopping on a plane, *Moya dusha* but I got distracted."

Just thinking about said distraction has my cock hardening. Not willing to greet my family with a hard-on I stop that line of thought and put an arm around Vincetti's shoulders. Kissing his temple, I lead him out the bedroom. "So, we're still waiting on your father?"

Vincetti nods. "He should've been here already but is probably dragging his feet. I doubt he's looking forward to facing my wrath again."

"Are you still mad?"

"I'm pissed and will probably remain that way for a while, but I've already said my piece and I won't be going off again. Unless he says something stupid. Then I won't be held accountable for my actions."

Chuckling, I kiss his temple again. "Let's hope he doesn't say anything stupid then. I'd hate to have to visit you in jail, *moya dusha*."

Vincetti grins at me and scoffs. "Jail? Please, as if I'd go. If I punch my father in the throat because he deserved it, not even my mother would turn me in."

"Remind me to never get on your bad side."

Vincetti laughs and pats my cheek. "Don't worry, *Tesoro*. You could never get on my bad side. Even if I were pissed at you, I'd never lay hands on you in anger."

As soon as we step off the last stair both my mother and sister launch themselves at us. Vincetti steps out of the way just in time to avoid them but they hit me with such force it takes effort not to land on my ass. Then, they hug me so hard I can barely breathe but I don't mind. I haven't seen them in so long it makes enduring the torture of not being able to breathe well worth it.

When spots start to dance across my vision, I grit out, "Can't breathe," and sigh happily when their grip loosens. After a few more minutes, they finally let me go. My mother takes my face between her hands and says, "It's so wonderful to see you, *L'venok*. We've missed you."

Smiling down at her, I say, "I've missed you too, mom." She and my sister both look even more beautiful than the last time I saw them. They could easily pass for twins if it weren't for my baby sister being five foot four to my mother's five-foot eleven height. They both have blond hair, blue eyes, and sharp features a model would kill for. Alice was a surprise result of a one-week-stand my mother had with a man she met in a bar.

You know, Tesoro, I distinctly remember you telling me a while back that the only important people in your life were myself and your mother. Care to explain why your sister didn't fall under that category?

Wincing internally because I'd completely forgotten that conversation, I respond using our link.

She does fall into that category, moya dusha. Alice is my baby sister and I'm very protective of her. No one alive who isn't standing here right now knows she exists and is related to me. She's only twenty-eight and in an enemy's eyes, her age and the fact she's a 'defenseless woman' makes her vulnerable to anyone looking to get to me through her. Keeping her a secret is the only way to not give any enemy I might have the opportunity to use her against me. Pieire threatened her when she was just a toddler and after that I kept my contact with them to weekly calls that couldn't be traced. I'm sorry I didn't tell you about her when we had that conversation, but I'm used to keeping her protected by pretending she doesn't exist it's a force of habit.

Out of the corner of my eye, I see Vincetti smile and am relieved. I know he only asked me about that conversation because he needed to know that hiding my sister from him until recently wasn't done out of a lack of trust in him but out of habit in order to keep my sister out of harm's way. My mother patting my cheek not so gently brings my attention back to her. The raised eyebrow clues me in to the fact she probably said something, and I completely missed it while talking to Vincetti. "Sorry, what did you say?"

She grins and laughs. "I asked you a couple of things. The first, to officially introduce us to that lovely man over there. The second, are we really safe now? Be honest."

I nod. "As safe as you can be. Pieire is dead so there isn't a need to keep running. There's a possibility a new enemy might pop up in the future but if that happens, I'll let you know, and you can take precautions to keep safe." Holding out my hand to Vincetti, I smile when he immediately takes it and returns to my side.

"Mom, Alice, this is Vincetti, my fated mate," then pointing to my mom and Alice, I say to Vincetti, "That's Carina, my mom and Alice, my sister."

Vincetti holds out his hand for a shake and says, "It's nice to meet you both." Instead of a handshake, Vincetti gets roped into a hug that lasts almost as long as mine did before they finally let him go. My mom pats his cheek and says, "Let's sit down. I want to know all about you Vincetti and how you met my son."

Smiling as Vincetti leads my mother and sister into the living room, I head into the kitchen to fix us all something to drink and snack on while we talk. As I'm finishing up the stack of sandwiches and pitcher of iced tea, I get an alert for the front gate. Checking the camera through the app on my phone, I see Vincetti's father has finally shown up and buzz him through then carry the tray of sandwiches, tea, and glasses into the living room. Kissing the top of Vincetti's head, I say, "Your father is here. I just let him through the gate."

Vincetti stands and says, "I'll meet him at the door," then exits the living room.

Placing the tray on the coffee table, I sit down beside the spot Vincetti vacated. Alice grabs a glass and fills it with tea then picks up a sandwich, finishes it in three large bites then grabs another. Seeing us watching her she raises an eyebrow. "What? I'm starving. The food on the plane was shitty and didn't fill me up and we were too excited to see you, so we didn't even stop to get anything to eat after leaving the airport."

Chuckling, I say, "Eat as much as you like. There's plenty."

Hearing footsteps, I look up and see Vincetti coming towards us with his parents hot on his heels. Vincetti is smiling so the apology his mother promised would be given must've gone off without a hitch. Standing, I loop an arm around Vincetti's waist and sit in the recliner, pulling him into my lap so his parents can share the couch we'd been sitting on. Once introductions are made and everyone has a glass of tea and a sandwich, conversation flows. Vincetti and I silently take it all in as our parents trade embarrassing stories of us and get to know each other better. Now that Pieire has been dealt with, I hope my mother and sister will consider moving closer to us. It would be nice to have them here where we can visit whenever we want and not have to worry about keeping our contact to a minimum to prevent a trace.

It's moments like this that have me considering retirement or at the very least a change in jobs. Seeing as I've yet to take on a hit contract since Vincetti and I met, it would be easy to put the word out that I was retiring and move into something else like security. If I did that, my only worry would be my past rearing its ugly head again. The situation with Pieire proved I was right to be concerned with staying in one location and while it was a coincidence that he stumbled across me the next time won't be. I know even if I retire I'll still have enemies that might come out of the woodwork in the future and threaten the peace I've garnered for myself but with Vincetti by my side I know we can handle anything life throws at us. So, I say let them come. We'll be ready and we'll make them regret their decision to come after us.

When the word gets out that we're a force to be reckoned with then the enemies who'd rather stay alive than seek out revenge will disappear, and we'll finally be able to enjoy our lives without constantly looking over our shoulder. Though, being able to relax doesn't mean we'll let our guards down completely because only idiots do that. It's when you least expect it that an enemy strikes. Until the day arrives where we no longer need to be completely wary of everything and everyone we'll remain vigilant. So, when that day finally comes our life together will truly begin and we'll spend the rest of our days enjoying it to the fullest. *I can't wait.*

Later on, after his parents are gone and my family is settled in guest rooms far away from ours, I join Vincetti in our bathtub for an evening soak.

Vincetti is seated between my legs with his back against my chest. He leans his head back until it rests against my shoulder and smiles indulgently. "Today was wonderful. I wish all our days could be like this. Filled with laughter, love, and fun."

"Me too, moya dusha. There'll come a day where we won't need to look over our shoulders or worry about where the next threat is coming from. Once you take over for your father and you make things legit and I retire from what I'm doing to move into something else, we'll be one step closer to being able to settle down."

Vincetti looks at me, mouth agape and eyes wide with shock that quickly turns to giddy excitement. "You're retiring?"

Grinning at him, I nod. "Indeed I am, *moya dusha*. I want to eventually start a family with you and when it happens I don't want to be taking off for days at a time or dragging you and our children around the world for jobs that would take longer to complete or end up making new enemies that'll come after you and the kids. That's not the kind of life I want for us and retiring is going to go a long way towards keeping you and our future children out of harm's way."

Vincetti narrows his eyes and asks, "You aren't pulling my leg about this right?"

"Of course not. I'm already well on my way to retirement. I haven't taken on a job since we met and have no desire to. A couple phone calls made to the right people will get the word out that I'm officially done being a hitman. Then, I can focus on getting a security business off the ground."

Vincetti turns so he can take my face between his hands and says, "Have I told you lately how much I love you?"

Chuckling, I kiss him softly. "Yes, but you know I never get tired of hearing it."

"I love you, *Tesoro*. You have no idea how happy it makes me that you're no longer going to be running headlong into danger without me by your side."

Stroking his cheek with my thumb, I say, "I love you too, *moya dusha,* and I swear if there's ever a time where I need to run headlong into danger I won't do it without you."

Vincetti grins and taps my nose with a finger. "I'll hold you to that. Now, I believe when someone retires a celebration is required. What do you say we get out of this bath and *celebrate?*"

The way he waggles his eyebrows when he says 'celebrate' tells me he's not talking about throwing me a party. Naturally, I respond with, "I say that sounds like a damn fine plan to me, moya dusha."

"Then let's get to it."

Laughing, I pull the plug to let the water drain then hold him to me with one arm and stand. Not bothering with a towel, I carry him into the bedroom and lay him on the bed where we spend the rest of the night celebrating my retirement in a spectacularly pleasurable fashion.

EPILOGUE
NO REST FOR THE WICKED
Vincetti

Three Months Later...

Rule # 12: *When you've got a bad feeling don't let anyone try and convince you you're imagining things.*

Today's meeting with my father has been a nightmare. For the past few weeks, shit has been going downhill. Shipments have been going missing along with some of my father's men. Last week, one of said men was found dead after apparently being tortured. Ever thinks a new enemy is surfacing and

I'm starting to think he's right. Only this time, it seems my father's organization is the target.

I keep telling my father we need to take precautions by tightening security and changing up the schedules on when we receive a shipment along with finding a new place to store everything. However, like always, the stubborn bastard refuses to listen to me. He says I'm paranoid, but I know I'm not. Something is going to happen and just like before when Pieire kidnapped me by the time we realize it it'll be too late.

Ever since I woke up this morning my stomach has felt like it's been filled with lead. I can tell something is going to happen, but I don't know when. It's got me on edge and arguing with my father about security throughout the entire meeting today hasn't helped any. We have another meeting now that this one has ended only it isn't being held in the pride house but at a very public restaurant in the city. It's a meeting with a potential new buyer that has been completely vetted. Thank the gods my father learned his lesson on that front after shit went down with Pieire. *Maybe when something happens to prove me right about security he'll learn his lesson there too.*

Being stubborn is fine until that stubbornness puts others in danger. A point that's proven when my father exits the pride house before me and the SUV waiting for us suddenly explodes. The force of it sends everyone nearby flying including myself and my father. Ever being as quick as he is saves me from hitting the floor hard. My ears are ringing and the heat from the blast is suffocating. It takes a minute to get my bearings because the ringing in my ears combined with the overwhelming scent of burning flesh, gasoline, and other things has me disoriented but once I have myself under control I start looking around to see if I can help anyone.

When my gaze lands on my father who's lying on the floor with a pool of blood surrounding his head, I'm frozen in horror but instinct kicks in and I race over to him. Checking for a pulse, I'm relieved to find he has one. Ripping off my suit jacket I ball it up and gently lift my father's head pressing the jacket to the back of it hard in order to stem the flow of blood until someone can help. I'd carry him to the clinic, but I'm worried he could have a spinal injury and the last thing I want to do is cause anymore damage.

Finally, after what feels like forever but was likely only a few minutes the pride doctor swoops in with an entire team of medical personnel from the clinic that splits off to help as many people as possible. They strap my father to a backboard after putting a c-collar on him and transport him over to the clinic. Knowing the doctor's team has everything under control here I head over to the clinic myself with Ever.

Once I've been checked out and learn my eardrums are busted but will heal themselves in a couple hours, I head to the waiting area where I settle in with my family to await news on my father. Hours later, my hearing is back in working order when the pride doctor comes out and hits us with news I never expected. Six little words leave his mouth and turn my world upside down.

"The alpha is in a coma."

The End (For now…)

I hope you enjoyed the second installment of Ever and Vincetti's story. As you can tell by the epilogue their journey isn't over yet. Keep an eye out for book three Love and Lethal hopefully coming to you sometime in 2021. Thanks for reading!

Continue reading for the blurb of one of my WIP's book eight in the Asphalt Bay Series titled

The Demon's Gruff Councilman

Coming Soon

Details of blurb subject to change

The Demon's Gruff Councilman

(The Demon's Gruff Councilman is a short story and part of a series. The Asphalt Bay and Venetian Hills books were written with the intention they'd be read in a certain order. It is recommended that you read all previous books before starting this one. Reading order can be found inside this book.)

Krealik

Krealik Putlova is a dragon shifter and council member. Having been the target of senseless violence years ago, he vowed to bring the hammer of justice down on those responsible. With the teams he oversees catching Carmine Verucci, Krealik believes he's one step closer to getting justice. Until Carmine dies and he's back to square one. When Krealik receives word that new information has been discovered he goes to hear it in person.

Belphegor

Belphegor is one of the demon princes of Hell overseeing his brother Belial's territory while Belial is off working for the council to shut down the labs. However, when an emergency pops up that he can't handle alone Belphegor goes to retrieve his brother. Only, he lands himself in the middle of an important meeting and his sudden appearance has the group perceiving him as a threat.

Together

Neither man expected to meet their mate that day, but it happens. With the emergency back home and the new information on the enemy being fought by Krealik's teams, these two will have their work cut out for them in order to achieve their happily ever after. Can they do it or will the challenges they face get in the way?

*(**Warning:** Contains sexual content and explicit language. Not recommended for those under the age of 18.)*

Dust—Tremonti

Save Yourself—My Darkest Days

Common Ground—Our Last Night

Sympathy—Too Close To Touch

Lifelines—I Prevail

If I Were—Nothing More

ACKNOWLEDGMENTS

I want to thank my parents for supporting me no matter what I do and tolerating me when I get in the zone of writing and ignore them completely. By tolerating, I'm really saying thanks for putting up with my shit. You have no idea how much that means to me. I love you guys. I want to thank Lisa Oliver, one of my favorite authors for encouraging me to write the story speaking in my head instead of forcing myself to stick to a different stereotype and for being an amazing friend I can bounce crazy ideas off of.

I want to thank Jemma Brown for designing such amazing covers for me. I thank the readers for taking the time to read a story from an unknown author like me. I want to thank my characters for coming to me when I was at a loss as to what to write/do next. Last, of all I want to thank all the musicians out there for playing their music and inspiring me.

ABOUT THE
Author

Well Ezra isn't my real name obviously, but I liked the name, so I decided to use it. I live at home with my five dogs and one cat. I started out writing hetero romance novels, but it wasn't where my heart lied. I adore all things paranormal and M/M is by far my favorite genre, so I decided to start writing Paranormal Romances. There's a guaranteed happy ending with each of my books even if it may take some time for my guys to get there. I love each and every character on the page as if they were my own children.

It sounds weird but that's how I feel about them. I've been writing for as long as I can remember but only started actively pursuing it as a career three years ago. Since I published my first book in 2014 I have written and released multiple books with many more to come. My current list of projects is longer than my arm, so I look forward to writing and creating new stories for my readers to enjoy.

OTHER BOOKS BY
Ezra Dawn

Standalones (M/F)

Playboy

The Crimson Deceit

Don't Fear the Reaper

The Boy Next Door

Standalones (M/M)

Paying for Love

Law of the Irish

Practical Ghosters

Abominable What-A?

The Cursed Prince

A Raven Walks Into A Bar *Spin-Off*

The Surgeon's Instant Family *Spin-Off*

Not A Snowball's Chance in Hell

Accidental Valentine

Poke His Bear

Asphalt Bay Pack Series (M/M)

An Alpha for the Demigod

The Enforcer's Secret Vampire

The Beta's Poison Bite

Taming the Feral Tiger

The Doctor's Demon Prince

The Leopard's Twin Troubles

The Warlock's Beautiful Bird

The Four Horsemen Collection (M/M)

The Four Horsemen

Azazel

Sen

Taz

The Graveyard Shift (M/M)

The Mortician

The Caretaker

The Director

The Florist

The Mistake *Spin-Off*

The Driver

Venetian Hills (M/M)

The Alpha's Master

The Second's Cursed Mate

The Beta's Second Chance

The Panther's Favorite Bully

Risqué Business (M/M)

Be My Prince

Seeking Rayne

Paranormals of Rockydale (M/M)

Misunderstanding His Mate

The Friendly Ghost's New Beginning

Forbidden Loves (M/M)

All is Fair in Love and War

The Submission Trilogy (M/M)

The Hybrid's Submission

The Wolf's Hybrid Dom

The Hybrid's Dominant Mate

Furry Tails (M/M)

Sugar and Spice

Crimson and Clover

Watson and Sherlock

Diary of a Hitman (M/M)

Blood and Bullets

Past and Poison *(You just finished it!!!)*

Planet Xenos (M/M)

The Heir's Vampire Guardian

Upcoming Releases:

Titles Subject to change

The Lion's Crown—TBA

Death and His Necromancer—TBA

CONTACT THE Author

You can find me on Facebook, MeWe, Twitter, and on my website.

Facebook: Ezra Dawn Author or Ezra's Book Groupies

MeWe: Amanda Ezra Ezra Dawn or Ezra's Asphalt Baywatchers

Twitter: @graveshadowcrow

Website: www.ezradawnauthor.com

I look forward to hearing from you!

Want updates on my new releases, WIP's, and exclusive giveaway opportunities? Sign-up for my newsletter by following this link and filling out the form.

Newsletter: www.ezradawnauthor.com/contact